This book belongs to:

The really REALLY Hairy Flight of SNARLY SALLY

written & illustrated by

Barbara Briggs Ward

LANDAUER BOOKS

PLEASE COME HOME SNARLY AND TANGLES. WE MISS YOU!

This book was designed, produced, and published by Landauer Books
A division of Landauer Corporation
12251 Maffitt Road, Cumming, Iowa 50061

President: Jeramy Lanigan Landauer
Vice President: Becky Johnston
Managing Editor: Marlene Hemberger Heuertz
Art Director: Laurel Albright
Graphics Technician: Stewart Cott

ISBN: 1-890621-23-4

This book is printed on acid-free paper.

Printed in China

10 9 8 7 6 5 4 3 2 1

Sally
had
beautiful
long
hair.

Everyone
loved
Sally's
hair.

Everyone
except...

...her
mother.

That's
because
every day
Sally's
mother
chased
her...

over the couch...

under the bed...

around the
kitchen
table....

After Sally
was caught
she would
wiggle
and
squiggle...
yell
and
kick
as Mother
brushed the
snarls out of
Sally's hair...

Sally hated
to have her hair
combed and brushed!

One morning after chasing Sally for a very long time, Mother sat down and said, "That's it! I'm not chasing you anymore.

YOU can take care of your hair.

I guess you will just be a Snarly Sally!"

And that is just what Snarly Sally did.

Every day her snarls grew

BIGGER...

and

BIGGER...

and

BIGGER!

“You look just like Tangles,”
the kids shouted.

Tangles was Snarly Sally’s little puppy. His ears were always a mess! Snarly Sally did not mind looking like Tangles. She thought it was fun!

One day while playing, a kite became stuck in Snarly Sally's hair. Along came a gust of wind! "Jump Tangles! Jump!" she yelled.

Snarly Sally held out her hand as she started to drift away. Up Tangles jumped and off they flew!

Through the clouds they sailed...

They were so high they could see way past Mother's garden.
They zipped past the playground.
"Look," Snarly Sally's friends yelled. "Look, it's Snarly Sally and Tangles!"
Snarly Sally waved. How small they looked below!
"I bet they wish they could fly with us, Tangles," Snarly Sally giggled.

Twinkling stars lit the sky as The
Man In The Moon tried to help.
"It's okay Mr. Moon," Snarly
Sally said as they floated by.
I LOVE TANGLES
STARS
STARS
STARS

The two friends had fun until—the kite ripped!

At sunrise
Snarly
Sally
could
see that
the kite
was
snagged
on a
branch
of a
very
tall tree.

She

tugged!

She

pulled!

But…
the kite
would
not budge!

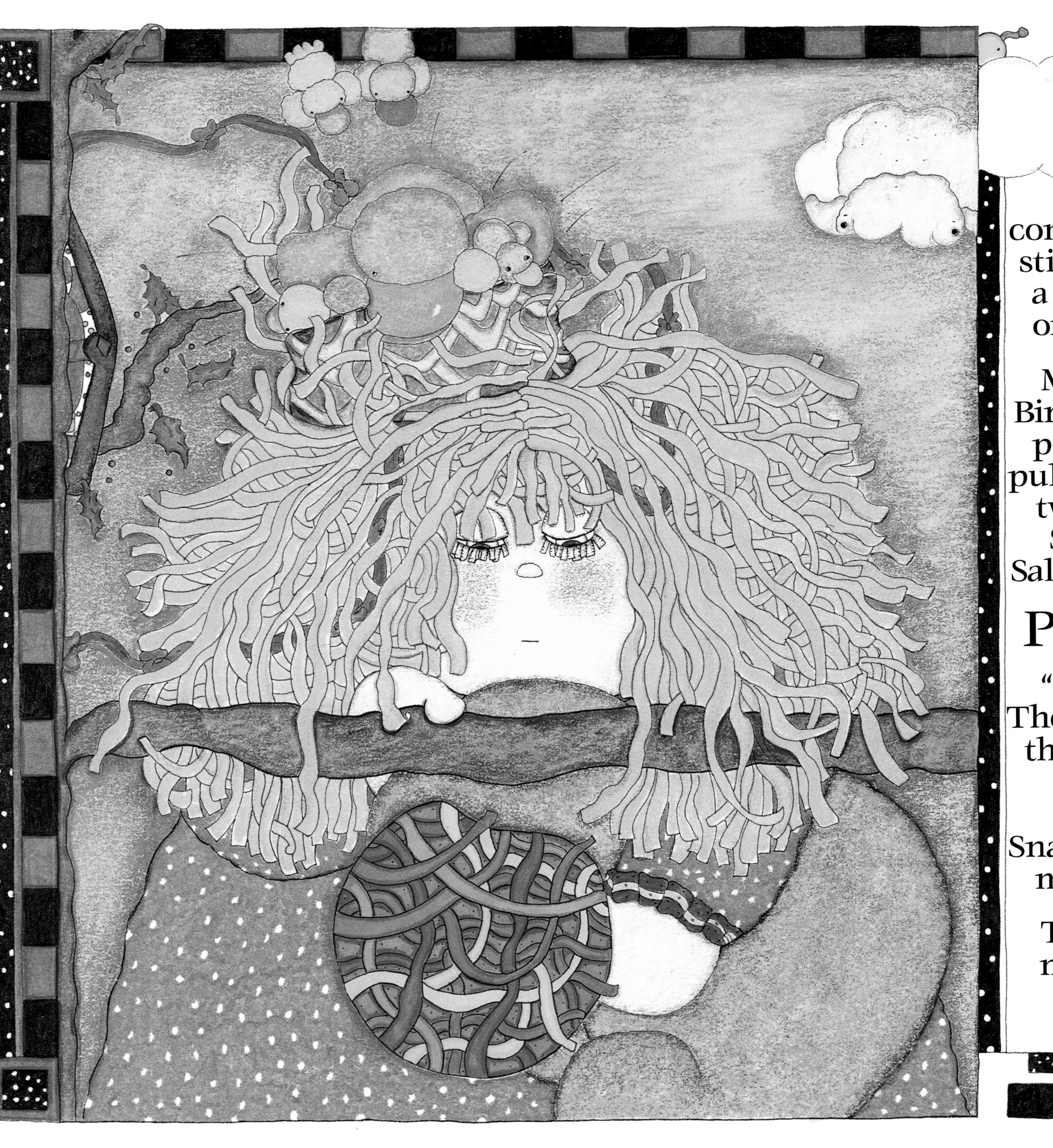

The commotion stirred up a family of birds.

Mother Bird began pecking, pulling and twisting Snarly Sally's hair.

PLOP!

"Oh no! They've put their nest in my hair!" Snarly Sally moaned.

Tangles moaned too.

The two friends dangled
from the branch.

The wind circled
Snarly Sally
making her hair
even messier.

Butterflies became
caught in Snarly
Sally's hair.

The birds in
Snarly Sally's
hair began to
chirp and Tangles
peeked up at them

The wind was so strong and her head was so heavy that the branch broke... sending Snarly Sally and Tangles through the air.
Hear the wind's song as it moves you along...
Feel the wind's hand as it glides you over the land.

OVER THE TOWN THEY SOARED!

An old lady tried to help, but her cane got stuck in the huge snarls.
Then whomp! A kid's kickball got stuck, too!
MY CAT
74

Flags
by Snarly Sally
Flapping...Swaying through the air!
I wish flags were everywhere!
Dodging a flagpole, Snarly Sally spotted her home. “Mother! Mother!” She hollered.
GEL
HAIR
COOKIES

Snarly Sally's Mother was in the garden.
Looking up, she could not believe her eyes!
"Catch us, Mother! Quick!" yelled Snarly Sally.
Tangles began to bark. He knew he was home!

Into the house ran Mother. Through the kitchen. Up one flight of stairs and another until she reached the attic! Out onto the roof she climbed. “Grab the rope,” shouted Mother. “And hold on tight!” Snarly Sally did. Tangles did, too.

Mother wrapped the rope around the chimney.

Down came Snarly Sally and Tangles.

The three hugged. "It sure is nice to be back home," Snarly Sally whispered.

Mother hugged them both a little tighter.

Mother
by Snarly Sally
Even though I
acted up and
didn't listen
to my Mother.
She will always
love me
She's really
like no other!

Downstairs Snarly Sally pleaded with her mother.

"Please comb my hair Mother! I won't run around or wiggle or scream!"

Snarly Sally stayed very still while Mother untangled...

...the kite, the ball, and the cane. The butterflies flew away! Mother Bird carried her nest to a nearby tree.

Sally gave her Mother a great big hug. "Thanks Mother. I like my hair much better this way.

You can have the snarls Tangles. They look better on you!" Tangles wagged his tail. He thought the snarls did too!

That night as Sally was getting ready for bed, she made a mess of snarls in her hair. Looking in the mirror, she grinned.

"My hair doesn't look that bad… I mean, we did have a lot of fun! Right Tangles?"

Tangles wagged his tail.

I LOVE SNARLY
I LOVE TANGLES
While the two friends slept, the stars twinkled and The Man In The Moon smiled.
"Rest up little ones," he whispered. "Who knows what adventure is next."
TANGLES
My Puppy Tangles
by Snarly Sally
He's so cute and cuddly as he rests from our fun-filled days.
I know he's dreaming about tomorrow and all the games we'll play!

Snarly Sally
and Tangles...

Friends Forever.

AIR
N DITIONER

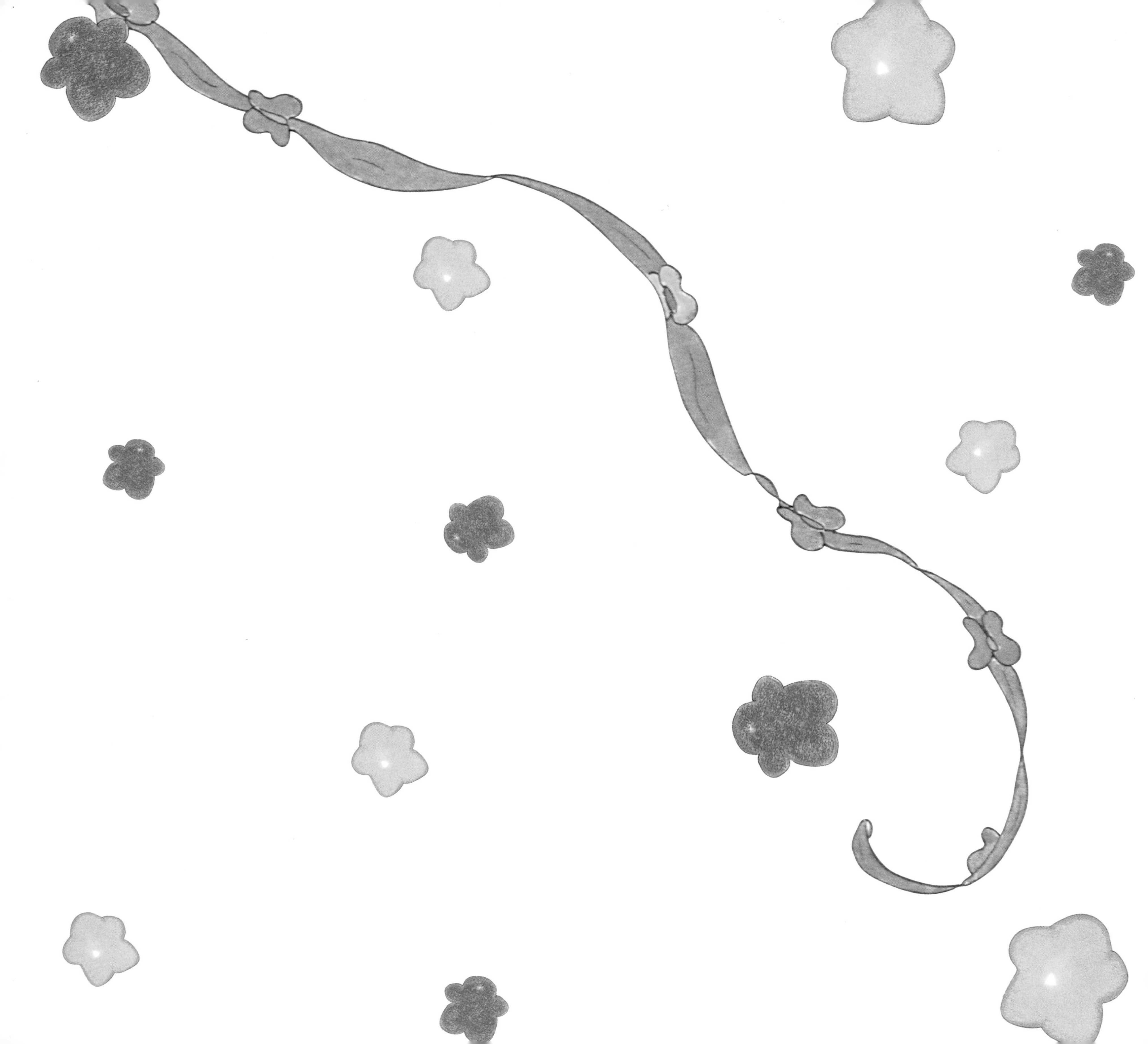